Hee haw haw

Thump thump thump!

Meow meow meow

Baa baa baa

Grump grump grump

Caw caw caw

Maa maa naa

Coo coo coo

**To
Kevin Moore–Murphy**

First published in Great Britain 1999
by Methuen Children's Books
an imprint of Egmont Children's Books Limited
Michelin House, 81 Fulham Road, London SW3 6RB

Copyright © Mary Murphy 1999
Mary Murphy has asserted her moral rights

ISBN 0 416 19607 1

A CIP catalogue record for this title
is available from the British Library

Printed in Olivotto, Italy

My Puffer Train

Mary Murphy

Methuen Children's Books

"Choo choo!" Here comes my puffer train.

"Puffa puff puffa" goes my puffer train.

Past a dog on a shed going "Bow wow wow"

and a cat on a pot going "Meow meow meow".

Past a plump pink pig going "Grump grump grump"

nd a fluffy white rabbit going "Thump thump thump!"

Past a cow in a field going "Moo moo moo"

and a dove in a tree going "Coo coo coo".

Past a big mama sheep going "Baa baa baa"

and a little baby lamb going "Maa maa maa".

"Choo choo!" There goes my puffer train.

"Puffa puff puffa" goes my puffer train.

Past a hen with her chicks going "cheep cheep cheep"

and a bossy old goose going "Beep beep beep!"

Past a donkey kicking up going "Hee haw haw"

and a scraggy old crow going "Caw caw caw".

Past seagulls in the air going "Kaa kaa kaar!"

All the way to the station going "Here we are!"

What a lovely day

to play in the sun.

Then "All aboard!" home again

going "Wasn't that fun?!"

cheep

Caw caw
caw

Moo
moo
moo

Coo coo
coo

Maa maa
maa

Bow wow wow

Kaa kaa kaar!

cheep